curvy girl for santa

emma bray

one

. . .

Anastasia

MY FINGERS DANCE over the keyboard, finalizing the donation request letters for our annual Christmas charity drive. The community center buzzes with activity as volunteers hang garlands and set up tables, and my heart is over-flowing.

This is what Christmas is all about.

"Anastasia?" Maggie, my co-organizer, pokes her head in. "You won't believe it. We got a massive donation for the toy drive. I'm talking life-changing money."

I blink, jarred from my reverie. "What? From who?"

She shrugs. "All it says is from a 'Secret Santa.' Whoever it is, they just made a lot of kids very happy this Christmas."

"Secret Santa," I murmur, a smile tugging at my lips. What kind of person can give so much and expect nothing in return? Even without a name, I feel drawn to their generous spirit.

"And that's not all. Someone else just volunteered to be Santa for the Christmas party." Maggie winks at me. "And let me just say, if his bod matches his voice, we are in for a treat. He's waiting for you in the main room."

My pulse quickens as I smooth my sweater over my curves. Why do I suddenly care what this mystery Santa thinks? I push open the door...and nearly burst into flames.

Holy mother of God.

Broad shoulders, a chiseled jaw—even in a Santa suit, the man steals my breath. He extends a large hand and I place mine in his, electricity arcing between us.

His blue eyes crinkle at the corners as he takes me in. "Anastasia," he says, like a caress, "looks like we'll be spreading Christmas cheer together."

"Hi," I squeak. "And you are?" I prompt for his name.

"I'm Ryan," he rumbles, holding my gaze. "Just a regular guy who wants to help out."

Regular, my foot. Everything about him screams power and confidence. I try to gather my scrambled wits.

"Well, Ryan, I'm so glad you're here." I flash him my warmest smile. "The kids will adore you."

"I hope so." His eyes dance with secrets.

He releases my hand and I feel bereft, aching for his touch. I turn abruptly to the decorations, my cheeks flushed.

"Shall we get started then? Lots of work to do to make the place merry and bright."

"My pleasure." The words roll off his tongue like an intimate promise. He takes a step closer, crowding me with his virile heat. "Just tell me what you want, Anastasia."

Everything, I nearly gasp. I want *everything.*

Trying to keep my voice steady, I direct him to the garlands. As we work side-by-side, hanging ornaments, our hands brush again and again, sending tingles through me.

I sneak glances at him, marveling at the sexy play of muscles beneath his red velvet coat. Who is

this gorgeous enigma? When he catches me looking, a slow, knowing smile spreads across his face.

I quickly avert my gaze, pulse galloping, but his
eyes stay branded on me. *Melting* me. The tension
between us simmers, thick and heady, flavored
with tantalizing possibility.

The hours slip by as we transform the space into
a winter wonderland. With each passing minute,
the pull between us grows stronger, a live wire of
desire thrumming just beneath the surface.

"You're a hard worker," Ryan murmurs,
suddenly behind me as I fluff the branches of the
massive Christmas tree. "I admire that in a woman."

His deep voice resonates through me and I
shiver, trying to ignore the images his praise
conjures in my mind—of working hard in a decidedly different context. "T-thank you," I stammer. "I
could say the same about you."

"Oh, you have no idea." His breath is hot
against my ear and I nearly combust. "The things I
could show you..."

I whirl around, a witty retort on my tongue, but
the words evaporate at the smoldering look in his
arctic eyes. He's so close I can see the faint shadow
of stubble along his jawline. I wonder what it
would feel like abrading my sensitive skin as he—

A low whistle interrupts my forbidden fantasies. "Wow, you two sure got a lot done! Looks great!"

Kevin, one of the volunteers, stands in the doorway, his eyes wide as he takes in the transformed room. Spell broken, I force a smile.

"Ahem." Kevin clears his throat from across the room, snapping us out of our charged bubble. "So, looks like that storm is getting pretty gnarly out there."

I blink, disoriented, and step away from Ryan's heat. Glancing out the frosty window, my eyes widen at the swirling white squall blanketing everything in sight. When did that happen? I've been so wrapped up in Ryan I didn't even notice the weather turn from flurry to blizzard.

"Wow, you're right. It's really coming down." A thrill chases down my spine at the prospect of being snowed in with Ryan, followed by a shot of apprehension. Spending the night alone with him could be dangerous. Deliciously dangerous.

"Guess we better bunker down and keep warm, huh?" Ryan winks at me, his meaning crystal clear. Molten heat pools low in my belly.

"I suppose so," I murmur, busying myself with straightening the ornaments. Trying desperately not to imagine all the sinful ways he could keep me warm.

Kevin shuffles his feet. "Um, if you guys don't need me anymore, I think I'll try to head out before it gets worse. I got my four-wheel drive outside, so I should be fine getting home considering how close I live."

Part of me wants to beg him to stay, to preserve some semblance of propriety. But the wicked voice in my head cheers at the thought of finally being alone with my Santa Charming.

"Oh, of course, Kevin." I paste on what I hope is a reassuring smile. "You go on home. Ryan and I will finish up here. Drive safe!"

He hesitates, eyes darting between me and Ryan. "You sure?"

"Positive," Ryan answers smoothly, his tone brooking no argument. "I'll take excellent care of Anastasia. Don't you worry."

Oh lord. The way he says it, like a dark promise, sends shivers cascading down my spine. I have a feeling he intends to do a lot more than trim the tree with me tonight.

And part of me thrills at the thought, but then there's that other part of me—that unsure *virgin* part of me—that hesitates.

Kevin lingers another moment, then shrugs.

"Alright then. You two stay warm. See you at the party!"

With a jaunty wave, he zips his coat and pushes out into the snowy night.

I turn back to find Ryan looking at me with a decidedly wolfish grin, and my stomach flutters.

Seemingly unperturbed by the news, Ryan simply grins. "I'm sure we'll find some way to pass the time. Right, Anastasia?"

The way he says my name, like a filthy promise, nearly brings me to my knees.

Lord help me.

two

. . .

Ryan

SHE'S A GODDESS. An angel of light and warmth, with curves that could bring a man to his knees. And fuck, do I want to fall at her feet and worship her. The way Anastasia moves, the gentle sway of her hips, the bounce of her perfect tits, it's driving me wild. I ache to strip off this ridiculous Santa costume and show her what a real man feels like.

I've known her all of five minutes but already, I'm lost. Ensnared by her goodness, her giving spirit. It radiates from her like the glow radiates from her like the glow of a crackling fire, inviting me closer, tempting me to bask in her light. But I can't let her see the darkness in me. Not yet.

I'm a selfish bastard for even thinking I could have her. That I could taint her sweetness with my jaded soul. But God, I want to. I want to paint her body with my kisses, unravel her with my touch until she's shaking and desperate, begging for release. I want to hear my name fall from her lush lips as I make her come undone.

Gritting my teeth, I force myself to focus on hanging the damn garlands, and not on the tantalizing hints of cleavage peeking from her sweater. It's going to be a long fucking night.

"Oh!" Her soft gasp snaps my head toward her. She's reaching for the top of the tree, stretching onto her tip toes, an ornament in hand. Her sweater rides up, revealing a strip of creamy skin.

I'm behind her before I can blink, crowding her space, breathing in her scent of cinnamon and woman. "Let me," I rumble. Plucking the ornament from her fingers, I lean over her to place it on the highest bough, my chest grazing her back.

She sucks in a breath and I suppress a groan. I wonder if her pussy is already wet for me. If she's imagining me bending her over the table and taking her hard and deep.

"Thank you," she whispers, trapped between me

and the tree. I should move. I *need* to move. But I can't. Not when she feels so fucking right in my arms.

Slowly, I settle my hands on her hips, thumbs stroking her softness. Her head falls back on my shoulder, a breathy moan escaping her.

"Anastasia." My lips skim the shell of her ear as I squeeze her hips, pulling her lush ass flush against my straining erection. "Tell me to stop."

She just whimpers, her hips rocking subtly against my hardness.

Fuck. Yes. I slip my hands beneath her sweater to caress the warm, satiny skin of her stomach. She trembles as I inch higher, grazing the lace edge of her bra. I cup her perfect tits, heavy and full in my palms as my fingers tease her nipples through the delicate fabric. They bead against my touch, straining for more.

I nuzzle into her neck, my lips searching for her racing pulse. She gasps as I find it, sucking hard, branding her with my desire. *Mine.* A primal need to claim her seizes me and I spin her to face me, my mouth crashing down on hers in a brutal, devouring kiss.

She meets me with matched fever, her sweet tongue tangling with mine as I plunder her mouth. She tastes like heaven and sin, and I drink her down like a man possessed. Desperate for more, I walk her backwards until her ass hits the edge of the table. With a swipe of my arm, I send the decorations scattering to the floor.

"Ryan," she pants against my lips, her voice husky with need. "What are we doing?"

"What we both want," I growl. I cup her face, forcing her eyes to mine. They blaze with untamed hunger, bright green flames licking at my control. "Tell me you don't feel this. This fucking heat between us."

She swallows hard, her tongue darting out to wet her kiss-swollen lips. "I...I feel it."

That's all I need to hear. I attack her mouth again, my hands roaming greedily over her lush curves as I grind against her, letting her feel exactly what she does to me. My cock is painfully hard, throbbing with the primal urge to bury myself inside her sweet cunt.

She whimpers into the kiss, her fingers clutching at the velvet lapels of my Santa jacket. I shrug out of the coat, letting it drop to the floor along with my hat. Then I'm back on her, my hands slipping beneath her sweater, skimming over her silky skin. She arches into my touch, chasing more.

"Fuck, Anastasia," I groan against the slender column of her throat. "Wanted my hands on you all damn day. Ever since I first laid eyes on you. What is it about you, gorgeous, huh? Wanted to tear that sweater off and worship these gorgeous tits."

She grinds her pelvis against my straining erection with unpracticed jerky movements.

But then another box behind us crashes to the floor, shattering the heated moment between us.

Anastasia jumps back and blinks up at me, eyes wide and cheeks flushed, chest heaving with each ragged breath.

"I...I'm sorry," she stammers, backing away and hurriedly straightening her rumpled sweater. "We shouldn't...I mean, I don't usually..."

Fuck. I scrub a hand over my face, trying to reign in my raging desire. The last thing I want is to scare her off by coming on too strong.

"No, I'm sorry," I rasp, my voice rough with need. "I got carried away. You just feel so damn good in my arms."

A pretty blush stains her cheeks and she ducks her head shyly. "I'm not...I mean, I don't have a lot of experience with..." She takes a breath. "With this," she finishes, gesturing between us.

My heart clenches. She's so fucking sweet and pure. And here I am, ready to despoil her over the goddamn Christmas tree.

I step closer, tipping her chin up to meet my

gaze. "We don't have to do anything you're not ready for, Anastasia. I would never push you." I brush my thumb over her plump bottom lip. "I just want to make you feel good. Worship this gorgeous body of yours the way it deserves."

Her green eyes darken with need, tongue darting out to wet her lips. "I'm just nervous. I've never felt like this before."

Comprehension finally dawns on me. "Anastasia, are you a virgin?"

Her cheeks flush and she bites her lip as she nods.

Fucking hell, there is a god.

I fell all the blood in my body rush south as I grip my cock painfully to keep from ejaculating all over myself at just the thought of being the first—no, the *only* one—to ever have this curvy beauty.

She's mine now. Plain and simple.

"Let me take care of you," I murmur, pulling her back into my arms. "Let me show you how good it can be. We'll go slow. And the second you want to stop, we stop. Okay?"

She nods against my chest and I feel her melt into me, surrendering to the desire sparking between us. Slowly, reverently, I slip my hands under her sweater again, savoring the feel of her silky skin. She shivers and arches into my touch, a breathy little moan spilling from her lips.

"That's it, baby," I encourage, my fingers skimming the lace of her bra. "Just feel."

I trace the scalloped edges, teasing her with barely-there caresses before cupping her perfect tits in my palms. They overflow my hands, soft and full and fucking made for my touch. I squeeze gently, molding her curves as my thumbs graze her nipples. They pucker and strain against the delicate fabric, begging for my attention.

"Ryan," she gasps, my name a plea on her tongue, and holy fuck I've never heard anything hotter. My name in her sweet voice…fuck, it's enough to make me nut right here and now.

"I got you." I nip at her ear. "Need to see you. All of you."

She nods shly, and with a growl of pure male satisfaction, I peel Anastasia's sweater up and over her head, revealing the most magnificent pair of tits I've ever laid eyes on. Full, heavy globes encased in delicate lace, nipples straining against the fabric, just begging for my mouth.

"Fucking perfection," I groan, palming her gorgeous curves reverently. "I could come just from looking at you."

Anastasia whimpers, arching into my touch,

and I can't hold back another second. I yank down the cups of her bra, freeing her bountiful tits to my hungry gaze. Dusky pink nipples, puckered and pebbled, crowned by pale, creamy flesh.

"Oh god, Ryan..." She tosses her head back as I lower my mouth to her breasts, sucking one aching peak deep. I lave her with my tongue, teasing the sensitive bud until she's panting and writhing against me.

Her hands scrabble at my shoulders, nails digging deliciously into my skin as I switch to her other nipple, giving it the same devoted attention. I could spend hours just worshipping her tits, losing myself in her supple curves.

"You taste so fucking good," I murmur against her breast. "Sweet ambrosia. I could feast on you forever."

Anastasia mewls, a desperate, needy sound that has my cock jerking in my pants. Fuck, I'm so hard it hurts, my erection throbbing in time with my racing heart. I grind myself against the juncture of her thighs, right against her molten heat, and nearly explode at the damp warmth I find there.

She's wet. Soaked through her panties, all for me. The knowledge makes me dizzy with want.

"Feel that, sweetheart?" I press my rigid length firmer into her softness, groaning at the friction.

"Feel how hard you make me? I'm fucking dying for you."

"Oh god...oh Ryan..." Her hips undulate against my cock and it takes every shred of my control not to rip her pants off and plunge into her right there.

My hands migrate from her breasts to her lush ass, palming the ripe globes possessively. I squeeze and knead, pulling her tight against my straining zipper as I grind into her, mimicking the act I'm dying to perform.

"Fuck, that ass," I growl into the fragrant curve of her neck. "Want to mark it, make it mine. Want everyone to know this juicy, perfect ass belongs to me now."

Daringly, I deliver a light smack to one cheek and she yelps, her eyes flying wide with startled pleasure. My mouth goes dry at the glazed, wanton look on her face. She likes that. My innocent angel wants to be claimed, dominated.

And fuck am I the man for the job.

three

. . .

Anastasia

HIS HANDS SCORCH MY SKIN, leaving trails of fire in their wake as he gropes my ass, pulling me flush against his rigid erection. I can't stifle the moan that spills from my lips, a desperate, wanton sound that hardly seems like it could come from me.

But that's the effect Ryan has. He makes me wanton, desperate, needy in a way I've never been before. His touch consumes me, burns through my hesitance until all I can feel is the molten ache between my thighs, the empty throb that begs to be filled by his thick cock.

"Ryan," I whimper, grinding my hips against his, chasing the delicious friction. "Oh god..."

He growls, a primal, hungry sound, and starts walking me backwards until my ass hits the edge of the table. With a swipe of his arm, he sends the decorations scattering to the floor. Tinsel and glittery ornaments rain down around us but I barely notice, too consumed by the inferno raging in Ryan's eyes as he stares down at me like he wants to eat me alive.

"Gonna spread you out on this table and feast on your pretty pussy," he rasps, his big hands already working at the button of my jeans. "Gonna tongue fuck your virgin cunt until you scream for me."

Oh god, oh god, oh god. This is really happening. Ryan, this gorgeous, dominant man is about to have me—shy, inexperienced me—right here on the community center table. It's wrong, it's dirty, it's...

It's exactly what I want. What I need. To be taken, claimed, dominated by this man until I can't remember my own name.

He tugs my jeans down my legs and I step out of them with trembling legs, leaving me in just my bra and panties. Ryan's heated gaze rakes over me, his pupils blown with lust, his chest heaving.

"Fucking look at you," he groans appreciatively. "A goddamn wet dream come to life."

I flush all over, unused to such blatant male appreciation. I start to cover myself on instinct but he stops me, pinning my wrists in one big hand.

"Don't you dare hide from me," he admonishes darkly. "I want to see every inch of this lush body. You're fucking mine now, Anastasia. My eyes only from now on, you got that?"

I shudder at his possessive tone, my core clenching with need. I can't speak. All I can do is whimper as Ryan lowers his dark head, his scorching breath fanning over my sensitive flesh.

His hands stroke down my sensitive sides to hook into my panties. With a quick tug, he rips them away, baring my most intimate place to his dark gaze.

"Fucking soaked," he growls appreciatively, his fingers delving through my drenched folds. "So wet and ready for me."

My hips buck off the table as he finds my aching clit, circling it firmly. Electric pleasure zings through my nerves, my thighs falling open shamelessly. I've never been touched like this, never known it could feel this good. I can't think, can't breathe—all I can do is feel as Ryan plays my body like an instrument.

"That's it, let me hear you," he coaxes darkly, his fingers rubbing faster over the swollen nub. "Wanna hear those sexy sounds as I make this virgin pussy mine."

"Yours," I agree mindlessly, my hips churning into his touch. "All yours, only yours! Oh fuck..."

He brings his other hand up to pluck at my nipple as he rubs my clit, the dual sensations rocketing me higher. I can feel an unfamiliar tension coiling low in my belly, pulling tighter with every stroke. I chase it desperately, panting and moaning wantonly.

"Ryan, oh god, something's...something's happening..."

"That's it, baby. You're gonna come for me." His fingers move faster, pressing harder. "Gonna come all over my hand like a good girl."

The coil snaps.

My climax slams into me, exploding through my body in shattering waves of ecstasy. I cry out, my pussy clenching rhythmically as I shake and tremble. Distantly, I feel Ryan groan, his fingers gentling on my clit to ease me through the aftershocks.

"Fucking beautiful," he praises roughly.

Ryan's fingers slow their torturous caress as I float down from my high, my body still trembling with the aftershocks of the most intense pleasure I've ever known.

Slowly, the haze of lust clears from my mind and reality comes crashing back in. What am I doing? I'm spread out half-naked on a table, with a man I just met mere hours ago. A gorgeous, dominant man who makes me feel things I've never felt before, but still—essentially a stranger.

Shame and uncertainty flood me and I start to sit up, trying to cover myself. "Ryan, I...I don't know if I can do this," I stammer, avoiding his burning gaze. "It's too fast, we barely know each other, and I've never..."

Strong hands grip my thighs, stilling my movement. I dare a glance at Ryan's face and the intensity there steals my breath.

"I know, sweetheart. I know it's a lot," he soothes, his thumbs tracing gentle circles on my sensitive skin. "We don't have to do anything more that you're not ready for. I would never push you."

Relief floods me, followed by a confusing pang of disappointment. I should be grateful he's such a gentleman, not wishing those magic fingers would keep taking me apart.

Ryan helps me sit up, his hands lingering on my curves. "But Anastasia, you have to know..." He cups my face, forcing my gaze to his. Molten need burns in the icy blue depths. "This isn't over. Not by a long shot. You're mine now. I've tasted your sweet nectar, felt your perfect body quake apart in my hands...I can't just walk away."

I shiver at the dark promise in his words, my oversensitized body responding with a fresh gush of desire despite my nerves.

He leans in close, his stubble grazing my cheek, his husky voice a seductive murmur in my ear. "I'm going to have you, Anastasia. All of you. I'm going to claim this virgin pussy and ruin you for any other man. I'm going to fuck you so deep, so good, you'll never want anyone else."

Oh god. Liquid heat pools at my core and I press my thighs together against the ache.

"But not until you're ready," he finishes, pulling back to look at me.

I swallow hard, a whimper lodged in my throat. How does he expect me to form words when he says things like that?

As if reading my mind, a wicked grin tugs at his sensual mouth. "For now though..." His hands drift down to the button of his black slacks. "I need to mark you. Show the world this sweet, innocent angel belongs to me."

With a swift move, he frees his cock from the confines of his pants.

And oh. My *God.*

My mouth goes dry as Ryan's thick, hard cock springs free from his slacks. It juts out, long and thick and intimidating.

I've never seen one in person before. How is that supposed to fit inside me? Fear and anticipation swirl in my belly as I stare transfixed at his impressive erection, watching a bead of moisture form on the swollen purple head.

"Anastasia." His deep rumble snaps my gaze up to his face. Hunger and something darker, more possessive, burn in his blue eyes. "I'm going to paint your tits with my cum. Mark you as mine. Would you like that, sweet angel?"

I can only nod, my reservations melting away under the heat of his dominant stare. I've never wanted anything more. "

He groans, a rough, animalistic sound. One big hand wraps around his thick shaft, squeezing the engorged flesh. The other finds my breast, kneading it firmly as he pumps himself with hard, fast strokes.

My eyes are riveted to the hypnotic sight of his hand gliding up and down his impressive length, revealing and then re-sheathing the ruddy head. It's the hottest thing I've ever seen. I can't look away, can't stem the needy whimpers spilling from my lips.

"Fuck yeah, those noises," he grunts, his hand moving faster on his shaft. "Keep making those sweet sounds for me, Anastasia. Wanna hear how bad you need my cock."

I'm panting now, my hips shifting restlessly on the table as I watch him pleasure himself. My pussy throbs, empty and aching. I've never been so turned on in my life.

"Tell me you're mine," he croaks.

"Yours," I moan mindlessly, arching into his groping touch on my breast. "Only yours, Ryan!"

"Fuck, I'm gonna come." His voice is a dark growl, barely human. "Gonna mark this creamy skin, baby. Paint you in my cum so everyone knows you're mine now."

I gasp.

With a roar, he explodes. Thick white ropes of his essence shoot out, splattering across my heaving breasts in warm, sticky lines. I cry out at the sensation, my pussy clenching as he coats my flesh in his musky seed.

"Fuck, look at you." Ryan milks the last drops from his cock, his eyes black with lust as he takes in the erotic sight of my tits dripping with his release.

"Filthy angel, all marked up for me. So fucking hot."

He smears his cum into my skin with his fingers, rubbing it into my nipples until they glisten obscenely. The depravity of it, the base possession...

I've never felt so wanton, so deliciously filthy. My whole body is on fire, burning with a need only he can quench.

"Ryan," I whimper, squirming on the table. "Please..."

I don't even know what I'm begging for. I just know I need more. More of his electrifying touch, more of the way he makes me feel—treasured and dirty all at once.

"I know, baby," he soothes darkly. "I'm going to take care of you, don't worry. Going to make this aching virgin pussy mine. When you're ready."

I bite my lip to keep from telling him I'm ready now.

four

. . .

Ryan

I DRAPE tinsel along the mantle, my gaze drifting to Anastasia as she reaches up to hang an ornament, her ass jiggling deliciously. Heat surges through me and I tear my eyes away, only to find myself staring at her lush curves a moment later. This vibrant, compassionate woman is getting under my skin in a way I never expected.

My hands itch to explore her body. I remember how soft her skin good. How good her pussy tasted.

Fuck, I want to bury my face in her auburn hair and breathe in her scent. I long to coax breathy moans from her full lips as I worship every inch of her. But I can't let myself get carried away, no matter how badly I crave her.

She doesn't know who I really am—that I'm no ordinary volunteer but a billionaire in hiding. If Anastasia knew the truth, everything would change between us. She might look at me differently, see me as just another wealthy playboy looking for a small-town fling. And that's the last thing I want.

I'm torn between my growing feelings and the web of secrets I'm spinning. I've never met anyone like Anastasia. She's so genuine and warm, with a captivating inner light. Being around her makes me want to be a better man, not the jaded tycoon I've become. But how can I let her get close when I'm living a lie?

"What do you think of this spot for the wreath, Ryan?" Her melodic voice snaps me out of my reverie.

"It's perfect. You have a real knack for this." I flash her a smile, hoping she can't see the hunger in my eyes.

"I just want everything to be beautiful for the families we're helping. They deserve some extra joy this time of year." She returns my smile, her emerald eyes sparkling with an enthusiasm that takes my breath away.

In that moment, I know I'm in trouble. Because despite all the reasons I should keep my distance, I'm falling for the angel in front of me. And I have no idea if I can catch myself before it's too late.

She's unlike any woman I've ever met—warm, compassionate, and dedicated to her community. And as much as I want to, I can't shake the feeling that revealing my true identity would ruin everything.

"So, Ryan," she says, turning the tables on me. "Tell me more about yourself. What brought you to our little town?"

I hesitate, weighing my options. I could lie—tell her some half-truth about needing a change of pace. But looking into her guileless eyes, I can't bring myself to do it.

"Truthfully, I needed a break from my old life. My work consumed me, and I lost sight of what was important."

"What kind of work do you do?"

Shit. I can't tell her who I really am. So, I hedge. "I work at an office." It's not a total lie. I do work in an office. I just didn't disclose that I happen to *own* said office.

Her expression softens, and she nods in understanding. "I can relate to that. Sometimes, our dreams take up so much of our time and energy that we forget to live our lives."

A comfortable silence falls between us as we continue decorating. I can't help but notice the way her hips sway as she reaches for ornaments, and I shift my gaze, willing away the growing arousal.

"You know," she starts, her cheeks flushing, "my biggest dream is to expand the community center. We could do so much more for the kids in this town, but funding has always been an issue."

"That's admirable, Anastasia. I'm sure you'll find a way to make it happen."

She laughs, but there's a hint of sadness in her voice. "I wish it were that simple. Even if I could secure the funding, I'd need a miracle to pull it off in time for next year's event."

"Stranger things have happened," I say, unable to help myself.

"Maybe for people like you," she replies, glancing down at her curvy body. "But for someone like me, well, a girl can dream, right?"

I frown. Is she really put herself down? Jesus Christ, does the girl not realize what a knock-out she is?

Nope. I'm not having this. My girl is going to know her worth. I'll make damn sure of that.

"Anastasia," I say, gently taking her hand in mine. Her skin is warm and soft, sending shivers up my spine. "Don't ever think you're not good enough. You're beautiful, inside and out. And as for your dreams, I have no doubt every single of them will come true." Because I will make it my mission to make sure they do. Anything my girl wants, she's going to get.

She looks up at me, her eyes shining with unshed tears. "Really?"

"Really," I reply, meaning every word. In that moment, I realize that Christmas miracles do exist, and one of them is standing right in front of me.

———

Anastasia

The more time I spend with Ryan, the more I find myself drawn to him. He's different from any man I've ever met. Sure, he's handsome, but there's something else about him that intrigues me. He's thoughtful and kind, always quick to lend a hand without seeking praise. And when he looks at me, it's as if he sees straight through the layers to the woman beneath.

It's both thrilling and terrifying.

As we put the finishing touches on the decorations, I catch Ryan's gaze lingering on me again. The intensity in his blue eyes sends a shiver down my spine, and I feel my cheeks flush under his scrutiny. What is it about this man that affects me so deeply?

"How about we take a break?" I suggest, needing a moment to collect myself. "I could make us some hot chocolate."

Ryan's face lights up with a boyish grin that makes my heart skip a beat. "That sounds perfect. Lead the way."

We head to the small kitchenette adjoining the main room. As I bustle around, gathering mugs and ingredients, I'm hyper-aware of Ryan's presence behind me. The space suddenly feels too small, the air charged with an electricity that crackles between us.

I focus on the task at hand, heating the milk and stirring in rich cocoa powder, cinnamon, and a pinch of cayenne for an extra kick. The aroma of chocolate and spice fills the room, wrapping us in its cozy embrace.

When the hot chocolate is ready, I carefully pour

it into two oversized mugs, topping each with a generous swirl of whipped cream. I turn to hand one to Ryan and find him leaning against the counter, watching me with a soft smile.

"You're in your element here," he remarks, accepting the mug with a brush of his fingers against mine. "It's like watching an artist at work."

I duck my head, pleased by the compliment. "It's nothing special, just a little recipe I picked up along the way."

"Don't sell yourself short, Anastasia. Everything you do is special."

We settle at the small table, sipping our drinks in companionable silence. The chocolate is rich and smooth on my tongue, the hint of heat from the cayenne warming me from the inside out. Or maybe it's the way Ryan is looking at me over the rim of his mug, his eyes dark and intense.

"Tell me more about your dreams for the community center," he prompts, setting his mug down. "What would you do if funding wasn't an issue?"

I lean forward, my eyes sparkling with excitement as I outline my vision. "I'd love to add a wing dedicated to the arts—music rooms, a dance studio, a space for painting and crafts. So many of these kids have incredible talents, but they don't have the resources to explore them."

Ryan listens intently, his expression thoughtful. "It sounds like you've put a lot of thought into this."

"I have," I admit with a sigh. "But sometimes, it feels like an impossible dream. I mean, look at me —I'm just a small-town girl with big ideas and no way to make them happen."

"Hey," Ryan says softly, reaching across the table to take my hand. His touch is electric, sending sparks shooting up my arm. "Don't talk about my girl that way. You're amazing."

My heart flutters at the way he calls me *his* girl.

I remember the way he looked earlier as he jacked off onto me, and my cheeks heat.

I look down, unable to meet his intense gaze at the memory.

I'm falling for Ryan. Hard and fast.

five

· · ·

Ryan

ANASTASIA'S CHEEKS turn an adorable shade of pink at my words. She has no idea how gorgeous she is, inside and out. I want to spend every moment showing her. Worshipping her.

My cock stirs as I imagine peeling off her cozy sweater again, revealing those lush curves that haunt my dreams. Laying her out on the table and feasting on her sweet pussy until she screams my name. Fuck, I'm harder than a rock just thinking about it.

I force myself to focus, aware that she's still talking about her dreams for the community center.

Her passion and dedication to this town only make me want her more. This woman was made for me. I just have to make her see it.

My thumb strokes the inside of her wrist, feeling her pulse quicken at my touch. The air thickens with tension, our gazes locked in a heated stare. I'm about to say to hell with it and pull her into my lap when a loud bang shatters the moment.

We both jump, the spell broken. Anastasia hurries to the ancient radiator in the corner, frowning as she inspects it.

"Damn, the heater's on the fritz again. Looks like we'll be decorating in the cold."

I barely hear her, too focused on how her ass looks in those jeans as she bends over. Jesus, I want to palm those round cheeks and grind against her until she feels how hard she makes me.

We continue working, but all the while, the temperature drops, goosebumps rising on Anastasia's skin. She shivers and rubs her arms. I'm at her side in an instant, wrapping her in my embrace.

"Let me keep you warm, sweetheart." My voice is a low rumble, laced with all the dirty things I want to do to her.

She melts into me, her soft curves fitting perfectly against my hard planes. I bury my nose in her hair, inhaling her sweet scent. Fuck, I could hold her like this forever.

But with her lush body pressed to mine, my control is hanging by a thread. If I don't get some distance, I'm going to end up bending her over the nearest surface and claiming her right here.

I pull back reluctantly, my hands aching with emptiness. Anastasia looks up at me from under her lashes, her green eyes dark with an answering hunger. Shit, she feels this too. This overwhelming need to consume each other.

We gravitate back to the tree, ostensibly to finish decorating. But really, I just need something to occupy my hands before I give in to temptation. We work in charged silence, the only sounds our mingled breathing and the rustle of ornaments.

Anastasia reaches up to place a star on a high branch, her tits bobbing with the movement. I swallow hard, my throat suddenly dry. Fuck, I want to run my tongue along the creamy column of her throat.

Anastasia turns to me and smiles, and that's when I notice it. A sprig of mistletoe above our heads.

Her eyes follow mine, and then her cheeks flush as she sucks in a shaky breath before looking at me again.

My heart pounds. This is dangerous. I shouldn't let myself fall deeper. But staring down at her flushed face, her lips parted invitingly, I'm powerless to resist.

I cup her face in my hands, my thumbs stroking her soft skin. "Fuck Anastasia," I growl. "I *need* to kiss you."

Then I capture her mouth in a searing kiss, claiming her with lips and tongue and teeth. She whimpers and winds her arms around my neck, pressing her curves flush against me. I groan into the kiss, my hands roaming her body greedily. I *have* to touch her. Have to feel her softness yield to me.

I walk us backwards until her ass hits the table. With one swipe of my arm, I send the mugs crashing to the floor, cocoa splattering everywhere. I don't care. All I care about is getting my hands on my girl.

I break the kiss to yank her sweater over her head, revealing those beautiful tits again. "Fuck, baby. You're so perfect. I can't. I'm sorry, baby, but I can't wait. I need you, honey. Please…" I'm speaking giberish, begging her. Hell, I'll get down on my knees and grovel if that's what she wants. I just need her. Need her like I need air to breath. The need to make her mine once and for all is over-whelming.

"Ryan," she pants, her fingers fumbling with the buttons of my shirt. "I need you too. Please..."

That's all the permission I need. I strip off her jeans and panties, leaving her bare and open for me. She's already glistening, her pussy weeping with arousal. Seeing my dried cum on her from earlier makes me growl with primal male satisfaction.

Mine.

I drop to my knees, throwing her thighs over my shoulders.

"Hold on tight, sweetheart. I'm going to devour this pretty cunt."

Then I bury my face between her legs, lapping at her like a man starved. She cries out, fisting her hands in my hair as I feast on her, driving my tongue deep. I don't hold back, eating her out with reckless abandon. Sucking her clit.

"Oh god, Ryan! Don't stop!" She grinds against my face, riding my tongue. I love how responsive she is, how completely she gives herself over to pleasure. I could spend hours worshipping this sweet pussy.

But my cock is throbbing painfully, desperate to be inside her. I give her clit one last hard suck and rise to my feet, looking down at her wrecked expression with raw male satisfaction. My girl is a needy mess, and it's all for me.

I free my thick length, stroking it as I rub the swollen head through her soaked folds. "Tell me you want this, Anastasia. Tell me you need my cock splitting you open."

"Yes," she sobs, trying to impale herself on my shaft. "I want it. Want you so deep in my virgin pussy."

"Fucking hell, baby, you keep talking like that you're going to make me bust before I ever get inside this sweet thing."

Anastasia whines needily, spreading her legs wider in blatant invitation. "Please Ryan, I need you inside me."

Her words unleash the beast within me. With a guttural growl, I notch the broad head of my cock at her entrance and surge forward, impaling her virgin depths in one fierce thrust.

"Fuck!" I roar as her tight walls grip me like a vice. She's so tight, so fucking tight around my thick girth. I have to grit my teeth against the urge to blow my load that very second.

Anastasia cries out, her spine arching off the table as I bottom out inside her, stretching her impossibly full. "Oh god, you're so big! I feel you everywhere!"

"That's it, take my cock sweetheart. Fuck, you're squeezing me so good." I start to move, drawing back slowly before slamming home again, over and over. Claiming her untouched body with deep, pounding strokes.

She keens, nails raking my back as she clings to me. I set a punishing pace, the table creaking beneath us with every powerful drive of my hips. My balls slap against her ass as I rut into her wildly, lost to the primal need to make her mine.

"You're mine, Anastasia," I growl against her throat, my teeth grazing her fluttering pulse. "This sweet cunt belongs to me now. I'm going to fuck you full of my cum. Breed this virgin pussy and make you swell with my child."

She gasped, shocked at my words, but I'm too far gone. Too in over my head over her.

Her pussy clamps down onto me, and it sends me into a frenzy. I hammer into her brutally, the lewd squelch of her dripping pussy filling the room. She thrashes beneath me, incoherent with pleasure as I use her body for my own gratification.

"Gonna come," I pant harshly. "Gonna pump this ripe little cunt so full of seed. Fuck, FUCK!"

My hips piston frantically, driving into her as deep as I can go. Anastasia screams, convulsing violently as her pussy clamps down on my pistoning cock like a silken fist as he comes on my cock. Swear to god, it's the best thing I've ever felt in my entire life.

With a roar, I explode inside her, my cock spasming as I shoot thick ropes of cum directly against her cervix. I grind against her, shuddering and grunting as I empty my balls in her fluttering depths, marking her from the inside out.

I collapse on top of her, both of us gasping for breath. My softening cock slips free in a gush of our combined fluids. Anastasia whimpers at the loss but I shush her gently, gathering her limp body into my arms.

I hold Anastasia close as we both come down from the intense high, our breathing gradually slowing. Her cheek rests against my chest, her body molded perfectly to mine like we were made for each other. And in this moment, with the scent of our lovemaking heavy in the air, I know that we were.

This girl, with her compassionate heart and zest for life, has completely bewitched me, body and soul. I've known her mere hours but already I can't imagine my world without her. It should scare the hell out of me, but instead, a sense of rightness settles deep in my bones.

I stroke her back soothingly, pressing a kiss to her tousled auburn hair. "You okay, sweetheart?"

She tilts her head back to look at me, her green eyes soft and sated, a shy smile playing about her kiss-swollen lips. "More than okay. That was...incredible."

Pride surges through me, along with a possessiveness so fierce it steals my breath. I did that. I wrecked her for any other man.

"Good. Because this was just the beginning. Now that I've had a taste, I'm going to be addicted to this sweet pussy." I punctuate my words with a sensual caress of her still quivering sex, making her shiver and burrow closer.

"Ryan..." she breathes, and fuck if hearing my name on her lips isn't the hottest thing ever.

I could bask in the afterglow with her forever, but reality starts to encroach, the chill in the room registering now that the heat of our passion has cooled. Anastasia cuddles into me, no doubt seeking warmth, and protective instincts rise up inside me. My girl is cold. Unacceptable.

I ease her back onto the table and grab my discarded shirt, draping it around her shoulders. It swamps her curves adorably. More importantly, it will keep her warm while smelling like me. My cock stirs at the sight of her wrapped in my clothes, broadcasting to the world that she's mine.

I quickly pull on my jeans and then scoop her up in my arms, carrying her over to the worn couch in the corner. I sit down with her cradled in my lap, grabbing a fluffy throw blanket to tuck around us. Much better.

Anastasia snuggles into my chest with a contented sigh that makes my heart swell in my chest. I wrap my arms around her tightly, marveling at how perfectly she fits against me, like a missing puzzle piece slotting into place.

We sit in comfortable silence for a few minutes, simply savoring the connection flowing between us. But as much as I want to stay cocooned with her forever, shutting out the rest of the world, I know we need to talk. I have to come clean about who I really am.

I clear my throat, but then she looks up at me with those breathtaking eyes of hers, and my words stick in my throat.

I can't ruin this perfect moment.

I'll tell her soon.

I promise.

six

. . .

Ryan

I SLIP out the back door of the community center, my heart pounding. Guilt gnaws at me as I picture Anastasia's radiant smile, her auburn hair glowing under the warm lights inside. She's busy hanging garlands, humming carols, completely unaware that I'm slipping out on her.

I scan the parking lot.

The sleek black Audi waits in the shadows. Frank, my driver, nods as I approach.

"Good evening, sir," he says, opening the door.

I slide into the plush leather seat, inhaling the

scent of success and power. "To the city, Frank. We have a deal to close."

As we pull away, I force thoughts of Anastasia from my mind. Her curves, her laugh, the way she makes me feel alive—I can't afford distractions. Not now.

I pull out my phone, scrolling through emails. "What's our ETA?"

"About an hour, sir," Frank replies.

An hour to transform back into Ryan Caldwell, tech mogul and corporate shark. An hour to bury the man who loves small-town Christmas magic.

I loosen my scarf, feeling constricted. "Dammit," I growl, tossing it aside.

My fingers itch to text Anastasia, to explain. But what would I say? Sorry I'm actually a billionaire living a double life?

I laugh bitterly.

The car weaves through snow-dusted streets, city lights bleeding into a neon haze. Anastasia's laughter echoes in my mind, a siren call pulling me back.

"Fuck," I growl, fists clenching. Her warmth, her curves—they haunt me even now.

I close my eyes, recalling the softness of her skin, the way her green eyes sparkle when she smiles. It's addictive, that authenticity. So different from the cold, calculating world I'm hurtling towards.

"Sir, we're approaching the tower," Frank's voice snaps me back.

I straighten, steeling myself. "Right. Thank you, Frank."

The car glides to a stop. I step out, the biting wind a stark reminder of the life I'm choosing. The glass facade of Caldwell Industries looms above, a gleaming monument to my success.

I adjust my tie, slipping on the mask of the billionaire tycoon. With each step towards those revolving doors, I feel Anastasia slipping further away.

"Mr. Caldwell," the receptionist chirps. "The board is waiting."

I nod curtly, striding past. My shoes click on marble, echoing through the cavernous lobby.

But even as I ascend to the cutthroat world above, her voice echoes in my ear. Her smile is in my mind's eye.

I grit my teeth, pushing the thoughts away. There's no room for small-town dreams in this glass and steel reality.

I step into the elevator, my reflection staring

back at me from the mirrored walls. My jaw clenches, eyes hardening. This isn't the man Anastasia sees—this is Ryan Caldwell, billionaire shark.

"Focus," I growl, adjusting my cufflinks. "Billions on the line. No distractions."

But her curves, that inviting smile...*fuck.* I slam my palm against the wall, the sharp sting grounding me.

The elevator dings, doors sliding open to reveal a bustling hive of activity. Phones ringing, heels clicking, the scent of ambition and designer perfume thick in the air.

"Mr. Caldwell." My assistant materializes, tablet in hand. "The Wang deal—"

"Brief me," I snap, striding forward. People part like the Red Sea, averting their eyes.

She falls into step beside me, rattling off figures. "Their stock dropped 3% this morning. We can leverage—"

I nod, mind racing. This is what I'm good at—the hunt, the kill. So why does it feel so hollow?

I picture Anastasia's guileless eyes peering up at me so innocently.

I falter, just for a moment. My assistant notices, eyebrow raised.

"Sir? Are you alright?"

I school my features, squaring my shoulders. "Fine. Let's crush this deal."

But as I reach for the tablet, all I can think of is Anastasia's warm hand in mine, guiding me through a world of genuine connection and joy.

I shake my head.

I push through the conference room doors, a predator entering his domain. Suits stiffen, eyes dart my way. The air crackles with tension and expensive cologne.

"Gentlemen," I purr, sliding into the chair at the head of the table. "Let's make some fucking money, shall we?"

The screen flickers to life, numbers and charts dancing across it. But all I see is Anastasia's smile, warm as sunshine on snow.

"Mr. Caldwell, our projections indicate—"

I blink, forcing myself to focus. "Cut the bullshit, Harrison. What's the bottom line?"

He stammers, caught off guard. "Well, sir, we stand to gain—"

"Not good enough," I snarl, leaning forward. My fingers itch to touch Anastasia's soft skin instead of this cold, polished table. "I want blood. I want their company gutted and served on a silver platter."

The room falls silent. I can almost hear Anastasia's disappointed sigh.

I grip the armrests, knuckles white. "Well?" I demand, voice low and dangerous. "Are you all just going to sit there with your thumbs up your asses?"

The meeting lurches into action, voices overlapping as they scramble to impress me. But I'm adrift, lost between two worlds. The cutthroat billionaire and the man who found peace in a small town's warmth.

Anastasia, I think, closing my eyes for just a moment, *what have you done to me?*

The boardroom erupts into a frenzy of voices and flashing screens. I'm drowning in a sea of profit margins and market shares, but my mind keeps drifting to the curve of Anastasia's hips, the softness of her laugh.

"Mr. Caldwell, your input on the hostile takeover?"

I snap back to reality, my voice a low growl. "Hit them where it hurts. I want their assets liquidated by end of quarter."

The words taste like ash in my mouth. I imagine Anastasia's face, disappointment clouding those emerald eyes. But I can't stop now. This is who I am. Isn't it?

"Sir, the paperwork is ready," my assistant murmurs, sliding a stack of documents across the gleaming table.

I grab a pen, poised to sign. But my hand trembles, Anastasia's image in my head.

She believes in seeing the good in people, in *doing* good to people. Second chances.

Fuck.

I slam the pen down. "New plan. We're going to save their company."

Shocked gasps fill the room. I stand, buttoning my jacket, heart racing. "Gentlemen, I believe we're done here."

I extend my hand to the stunned CEO of said commpany across the table. He grasps it, relief flooding his features.

"Thank you, Mr. Caldwell. I don't know what to say."

I force a smile, but inside, I'm aching to be back in that small town, wrapped in Anastasia's arms. This victory feels hollow, empty.

"Don't thank me yet," I mutter. "We've got work to do."

As congratulations erupt around me, all I can think of is Anastasia and getting back to her.

I stride out of the conference room, my mind already miles away. The glossy corridors feel suffocating, each step taking me further from her. Anastasia's warmth, her curves, her infectious laugh—they haunt me, making this world of glass and steel feel like a prison.

"Mr. Caldwell!" My assistant's voice cuts through my reverie. She hurries toward me, arms laden with documents. "These need your immediate attention—"

"Not now," I growl, waving her off. The thought of more paperwork makes my skin crawl. All I want is to feel Anastasia's soft skin under my fingertips, to bury my face in her auburn hair and forget this façade.

My assistant's eyes widen. "But sir, the merger—"

"Can wait," I snap, jabbing the elevator button. The doors slide open and I step inside, my reflection in the mirrored walls a stranger to me.

As the elevator descends, so does the weight of my deception. I lean against the cool metal, closing my eyes. Anastasia's face swims before me—those captivating green eyes, that inviting smile. God, what I wouldn't give to taste those lips right now.

"Fuck," I mutter, running a hand through my hair. I *need* her. The urge to get back to her is a physical ache now.

As the doors open, I make a silent vow. No

more secrets. No more lies. It's time to show Anastasia who I really am—and pray she'll still want me when she knows the truth.

I stride through the lobby, my footsteps echoing on the polished marble. The revolving door spins, and a gust of frigid air hits me like a slap. I inhale deeply, savoring the bite of winter. It clears my head, washing away the stifling atmosphere of the boardroom.

My heart pounds, each beat screaming Anastasia's name. I'm a man possessed, consumed by the need to see her, to touch her lush curves, to lose myself in her warmth.

The sleek black car idles at the curb. I slide into the backseat, my voice husky as I order, "Back to the community center."

As we pull away from the curb, I close my eyes, allowing myself to indulge in the fantasy of Anastasia. Her melodious laugh echoes in my mind, sending shivers down my spine. I imagine running my fingers through her silky auburn hair, breathing in her intoxicating scent.

"Fuck," I growl, adjusting myself in my seat. This woman has me wound tighter than any multi-billion dollar deal ever could.

I picture her green eyes, sparkling with mischief as she teases me. Her full lips, curved in that irresistible smile. The way her sweaters hug her delicious curves, leaving me aching to explore every inch of her.

My fists clench at my sides. Soon, I promise myself. Soon I'll confess everything, consequences be damned. Because a life without Anastasia isn't a life worth living.

The car slows as we approach the center, and I start to breathe again. I'll see her soon, and then I can calm.

I step out, the crisp air shocking my senses. My gaze locks onto the building, knowing she's inside. My body thrums with need, every cell screaming her name.

"Ryan!" Anastasia's voice rings out, pure sunshine in this winter landscape.

I turn, drinking her in. She's bundled up in a emerald sweater that makes her eyes pop, snowflakes caught in her hair like a crown.

"Where'd you disappear to?" she asks, brow furrowed with concern.

I stride toward her, fighting the urge to crush her to me. "Just had to make a quick call," I lie smoothly, hating myself for it. "Couldn't stay away for long, though. Not when you're here."

Her cheeks flush, and I want to taste that blush. "Flatterer," she teases, but I see the heat in her gaze.

I take her hand, relishing its softness. "How about we grab some hot chocolate?"

As we walk, her curves brush against me. It takes every ounce of control not to pin her against the nearest wall and claim her lips.

Soon, I vow silently. Soon, I'll tell her everything. But for now, I'll savor this moment, this slice of heaven with my curvy angel.

seven

. . .

Anastasia

I GRAB RYAN'S HAND, pulling him into the department store. We're shopping for gifts for all the kids, and it couldn't be any more natural.

He holds my hand and periodically places a protective palm against the small of my back when we pass by other men. I even catch him glaring at those of them whose gazes linger too long, and maybe I should be offended by his possessiveness, but I'm not.

I love it.

"You know, I had an idea," Ryan suddenly says.

I look up at him.

"What's Santa without his helper help?" he says with a raised eyebrow as his gaze rakes over me and then to the racks of holiday attire.

I laugh as he grabs my hand and leads me over to the holiday outfits. My heart races as Ryan's fingers brush my lower back. The heat of his touch sears through my sweater.

"Let's try this one," he murmurs as he grabs a sexy elf costume from the rack. Our eyes lock as he takes it, electricity crackling between us.

He hands me the outfit. "Why don't you try it on for me?"

I bite my lip and blush at the suggestive look in his eyes.

He follows me to the dressing room and waits outside as I put on the costume.

I suddenly feel nervous at how revealing the costume is. My tits are pushed up on display and the form-fitting top shows off all my curves. The skirt barely covers my full ass, but I take a deep breath and open the door.

Ryan's eyes about bug out of his head, and I blush with satisfaction as I see the prominent bulge that instantly rises in his pants.

"Jesus, Anastasia," he croaks, and then quick as

a wink, he pushes me back into the dressing room and slips inside with me.

"Ryan!" I gasp as he presses me against the wall. His lips crash into mine, hungry and insistent. I melt into him, returning the kiss with equal fervor.

His hands roam my curves as I run my fingers through his tousled hair. Our breaths come in ragged pants.

"We shouldn't..." I whisper halfheartedly.

"Do you want me to stop?" Ryan asks, voice husky.

"God, no," I groan, pulling him closer.

We lose ourselves in a frenzy of heated kisses and roaming hands, the tiny dressing room amplifying our passion.

"Can you be quiet, baby?" he whispers, his breath hot against my ear as his lips slide down to kiss my neck.

I nod and stifle a moan.

"Good girl," he praises me.

Ryan's finger hooks the neckline of the skimpy costume, pulling it down to expose one of my breasts. The cool air makes my nipple pucker instantly. He groans approvingly before taking it into his hot mouth. I arch into him, biting my lip to keep from crying out.

His free hand snakes under the short skirt, squeezing my ass. A finger slips under my panties, teasing my slick entrance. I whimper and grind against him, desperate for more.

"Fuck, you're so wet for me already," he growls. In one smooth motion, he yanks my panties down. They fall to my ankles.

Ryan drops to his knees. He nuzzles his face between my thick thighs, inhaling deeply. "I've been craving this sweet pussy all day."

Then his mouth is on me, licking and sucking, coaxing gasps from my lips that I try to muffle with my hand. My other hand fists in his hair, pressing him closer. His stubble scrapes deliciously against my sensitive skin. Pleasure coils tight in my core as his wicked tongue drives me to the brink.

Just as I'm about to explode, he pulls back. I whine at the loss of contact but it turns into a gasp as he stands and spins me to face the mirror. My ass presses against the hard ridge of his erection.

Our eyes meet in the reflection, pupils blown with lust. He kicks my feet further apart and hitches my skirt up around my waist. I watch, panting, as he unzips his fly and frees his thick cock.

"Watch," he commands darkly. "Look at how good you look impaled on my cock, baby."

I moan wantonly as he notches his blunt head at my entrance. With one powerful thrust, he sheaths himself to the hilt. I scream into my palm at the sudden fullness stretching me. He sets a relentless pace, pounding into my dripping cunt.

The dressing room fills with the obscene slapping of flesh and our harsh breaths. I'm lost to the intensity of his possession, reduced to breathy whines as he takes what's his.

"Come on my cock," he snarls in my ear, pinching my clit. "Let me feel this greedy cunt milk me."

His filthy words send me hurtling over the edge. My pussy spasms around him as I come undone. He follows me with a deep groan, coating my fluttering walls with his hot seed.

We slump against the mirror, chests heaving. Ryan peppers kisses along my neck as we bask in the afterglow, still joined.

Eventually we emerge, flushed and disheveled. As we pay for the elf costume, Ryan's hand lingers on my waist.

After our thrilling tryst in the dressing room, we finish our shopping in a hormonal haze until Ryan's arms are laden with bags.

"Come back to my cabin," he murmurs in my ear.

Anticipation coils in my belly as I nod.

———

At his secluded cabin, a fire crackles invitingly. Ryan pulls me onto the plush rug, capturing my lips in a searing kiss. I thread my fingers through his hair as he trails kisses down my neck.

Our kisses grow more urgent, hands exploring with newfound intimacy. The firelight dances across Ryan's chiseled features as he gazes at me with unmistakable desire.

I've never felt so alive, so wanted. As passion consumes us, I know nothing will ever be the same.

This man has changed me, and I want nothing but him.

Ryan's strong hands grip my hips, effortlessly lifting me onto his lap. My curves mold against his hard body as our lips reconnect, hungry and desperate. His tongue sweeps into my mouth, tasting of cinnamon and desire.

"Anastasia," he growls, voice rough with need. "You're driving me wild. I can't think of anything but you, beautiful. Need you twenty-four hours a fucking day."

I whimper, grinding against him. "I want you, Ryan. So much."

His fingers trail fire along my skin as he slowly unbuttons my sweater. Each newly exposed inch makes me shiver with anticipation.

"You're breathtaking," he murmurs, blue eyes dark with lust.

The heat from the fireplace caresses my bare skin, but it's nothing compared to the inferno building between us. I arch into his touch, thoughts hazy with pleasure.

His lips blaze a trail down my neck as the last button comes undone. I moan, lost in sensation.

Ryan slowly peels my sweater off my shoulders, exposing my heaving breasts encased in black lace. His hungry gaze sears into me, igniting every nerve ending.

"Fuck, baby, look at you," he groans. Large hands cup my tits, thumbs brushing over my pebbled nipples through the flimsy fabric. I gasp, arching into his touch.

I fumble with the buttons of his shirt, desperate to feel his skin against mine. He helps shrug it off and I rake my nails down his sculpted chest, reveling in his sharp intake of breath.

"You're going to be the death of me," Ryan growls before sealing his lips over mine in a bruising kiss. I open for him instantly, our tongues tangling in a sensual dance.

I grind against the thick bulge straining his pants, soaking my panties with my arousal. He groans into my mouth, gripping my ass to press me harder against him.

"I need you," I pant. "Please, Ryan..."

In a flash, he flips me onto my back on the plush rug. The firelight flickers across his chiseled body as he looms over me, eyes smoldering with raw desire. I've never felt so wanted, so consumed.

He makes quick work of my bra, freeing my aching breasts. I cry out when he takes a nipple into his hot mouth, swirling his tongue around the sensitive bud. His hand kneads my other breast, rolling the nipple between clever fingers.

"Ryan, yes!" I moan shamelessly, fisting my hands in his thick hair to hold him to me. He lavishes my tits with attention, sucking and nipping until I'm writhing beneath him.

His lips travel down my quivering stomach, leaving a trail of fire in their wake. He nuzzles the soft curve of my belly before hooking his fingers in the waistband of my leggings.

Ryan peels them down my thick thighs along with my drenched panties, spreading my legs wide. I flush under his intensely appreciative stare, juices seeping onto the rug.

"Gorgeous," he rumbles. "My favorite dessert."

Then his face is buried between my thighs and I nearly scream at the first swipe of his tongue through my folds. He groans at the taste of me, lapping eagerly. Sparks shoot up my spine as he focuses on my swollen clit, sucking it into his mouth.

"Oh fuck, don't stop!" I sob, undulating my hips against his face.

He releases my clit to thrust his tongue inside my weeping entrance, fucking me with it. I thrash my head at the exquisite pleasure, seeing stars. He licks and sucks, working me into a frenzy.

Two fingers plunge into my soaked channel, curling to stroke my g-spot as he suckles my clit. The dual sensations make my back bow off the rug, a hoarse scream ripping from my throat.

"That's it, baby. Let me hear you," Ryan rasps against my pussy. "Come all over my tongue."

His filthy encouragement and relentless ministrations send me flying apart. I convulse, thighs clamping around his head as I gush into his eager mouth. He laps up every drop, prolonging my intense orgasm until I collapse, boneless and gasping.

"I'm going to eat this pussy every day," he growls, crawling up my body. His lips claim mine in a searing kiss and I moan at the taste of my essence on his tongue.

"I need you inside me, Ryan. Now," I whimper desperately.

"Fuck yes," he growls.

He stands just long enough to shed his pants and boxer briefs. My mouth goes dry at the sight of his impressive erection bobbing against his chiseled abs, the thick head glistening with precum. I lick my lips hungrily.

Ryan settles back between my splayed thighs, the blunt tip of his cock nudging my entrance. We both groan at the contact, the air crackling with tension.

His darkened blue eyes bore into mine as he notches himself at my opening. "You're mine, Anastasia. This sweet cunt belongs to me."

"Yes, yours! Please..." I mewl, trying to impale myself on his thick shaft.

With a possessive snarl, he snaps his hips and buries himself to the hilt in one powerful thrust. I cry out, back arching off the rug at the sudden invasion stretching me. He's huge, splitting me open so deliciously.

Ryan sets a punishing rhythm, sawing in and out of my dripping pussy with deep, pounding strokes. The wet slapping of flesh and our harsh panting fills the room.

"Fuck, you're so tight. Squeezing my cock like a vice," he grunts, angling his hips to go even deeper.

"Ah! Oh god, Ryan!" I keen, seeing stars as he hits that magic spot inside me over and over. My nails rake down his flexing back, surely leaving marks.

He bends to take a nipple into his mouth, biting down just shy of pain. I thrash beneath him, lost to the intensity of his possession.

"You take my cock so good, baby. Fucking made for me," Ryan growls around my breast. He wedges a hand between our sweat-slicked bodies, finding my swollen clit. I nearly convulse when he pinches the sensitive nub.

"I'm so close! Don't stop!" I wail.

"Come for me, Anastasia. Let me feel this perfect pussy milk my cock," Ryan commands, voice rough with strain as he fights his own impending release.

He rolls my clit between his fingers, flicking the sensitive bundle of nerves in time with his relentless thrusts. It's too much, the dual sensations hurtling me towards the edge at breakneck speed.

"Ryan!" I scream, my pussy clenching around him like a vise as I detonate. Wave after wave of mind-numbing ecstasy crashes over me, my entire body quaking with the force of my orgasm.

"Fuck yes, just like that," he snarls, pistoning his hips furiously to work me through the aftershocks. The obscene sound of my cream squelching around his driving cock only heightens my pleasure.

With a guttural groan, Ryan buries himself to the hilt one last time before pulsing deep inside me, painting my clenching walls with thick ropes of his seed.

"Mine," he growls, sinking his teeth into the junction of my neck and shoulder to mark me as he spills into my still fluttering cunt.

I keen at the pleasurable pain, trembling as he fills me to the brim with his release. We cling to each other, chests heaving, hearts pounding in sync as we float down from our mutual high.

Ryan gentles his grip, peppering tender kisses across my face.

I cup his chiseled jaw, gazing up at him adoringly.

"I'm going to take care of you. You know that, right, baby?" he tells, his voice and eyes serious as he gazes down at me with that smoldering intensity.

My exhausted pussy clenches weakly at his declaration, a whimper escaping my kiss-swollen lips. Ryan chuckles, the sound a sinful rumble against my over-sensitized skin.

Slowly, reluctantly, he withdraws from my well-used sheath. We both hiss at the sensation, already mourning the loss of our connection. Evidence of our coupling trickles out of me, the primal sight making his spent cock twitch against my thigh.

Ryan scoops me up bridal style, carrying me to the plush fur rug in front of the hearth. He lays me down with the utmost care, settling behind me to spoon my curves against his firm body.

I hum contentedly, basking in his warmth and the heat from the crackling fire. His fingertips dance across my skin, leaving goosebumps in their wake.

"I could stay here forever, just like this," I murmur dreamily, threading our fingers together over my stomach. "You make me feel

"I could stay here forever, just like this," I murmur dreamily, threading our fingers together over my stomach. "You make me feel so safe and cherished. Like nothing else matters but this moment right here with you."

Ryan nuzzles into my neck, his stubble deliciously abrading my sensitive skin. "You are cherished, Anastasia. And I'll make you feel that way every single day if you let me."

My heart flutters wildly in my chest at his heartfelt declaration. I twist in his arms to face him, our noses nearly touching with our proximity. Vulnerability and raw honesty shine in his striking blue eyes.

"I'm not going anywhere," I whisper, sealing my promise with a tender kiss. "You've completely swept me off my feet, Ryan. I'm all yours."

His answering smile is blinding before he claims my mouth in a searing kiss, passion instantly reigniting between us. Large hands skim down my curves to grip my hips, effortlessly shifting me to straddle his lap without breaking our liplock.

I moan into his mouth when I feel his hardening length pressing insistently against my bare bottom. Slick arousal coats my inner thighs as he grows fully erect, nestled between my cheeks.

"Again?" I tease breathlessly when we part for air, undulating my hips to slide my wet folds along his rigid shaft. We both groan at the delicious friction. "Insatiable man."

"I'll never get enough of this perfect body," Ryan rasps, kneading the globes of my ass. "I plan to spend days on end just like this, worshipping every inch of you until you don't even remember your own name."

Whimpering needily, I reach between us to grasp his thick cock, aligning him with my entrance. The broad head parts my soaked petals, making us both hiss.

Slowly, I sink down onto his impressive length, savoring the stretch as he fills me inch by glorious inch. I relish the burn, taking him so deeply I swear I can feel him in my throat. My walls flutter around his girth, drawing him in further until I'm fully seated in his lap.

"Fuck, you feel incredible," Ryan grits out through clenched teeth, fighting the urge to thrust up into my tight heat. "Like hot silk gripping me so good. Made for my cock."

"Yes, only yours," I agree breathlessly, beginning to rock on him. My hands splay across his chiseled chest for leverage as I find a rhythm, rising and falling on his thick shaft.

"Yes, look at you, you fucking good girl. Riding my cock so good. Take it, baby. Take what you need."

Ryan's words encourage me, and I grow bolder, giving myself over to what feels good.

His grip on my hips tightens, guiding my movements as he meets each downward grind with a powerful upward surge, spearing into me so deep I see stars.

"Yes, fuck, just like that!" I keen, head thrown back in ecstasy as I bounce on his cock with wild abandon. My tits jiggle with every thrust, the sight making Ryan growl possessively.

He sits up suddenly, changing the angle so he's hitting that magic spot inside me with every stroke. I cry out sharply, my hands flying to his shoulders to anchor myself as the new position allows him to plunge even deeper.

"That's it, squeeze my cock," he grunts, peppering my neck with biting kisses that are sure to leave marks. "Gonna fill this pussy up again, pump you full of my cum."

I clench around him at his filthy promise, my arousal spiking. "Please, Ryan! I need it, need you to breed me," I wail shamelessly, too far gone to care how wanton I sound.

That drives him crazy. He lets out a feral grown and wraps his arms around me, fucking into me harder, faster.

"Fuck yes, gonna knock you up with my baby," Ryan snarls, his own control slipping. He snaps his hips up brutally, the force lifting me clear off his lap only to slam me back down.

Our bodies move together in a carnal dance, the wet sounds of our coupling mixing with skin slapping against skin and our harsh panting. My blood roars in my ears, my entire being focused on the thick shaft splitting me open so exquisitely.

"Ryan, I'm so close!" I gasp, my walls beginning to flutter around him. The telltale tingle starts at the base of my spine, pleasure coiling tighter and tighter.

"Me too, baby. Let go, come with me. Come all over my cock," he demands roughly, snaking a hand between us to rub tight circles on my engorged clit.

The added stimulation catapults me over the edge and I detonate with a silent scream, my cunt clamping down on him like a vise as I gush around his pistoning length. Stars burst behind my eyelids, my body convulsing with the intensity of my release.

"Fuck, yes! That's it, Anastasia!" Ryan roars, slamming into me one last time before erupting, painting my spasming walls with thick ropes of his hot seed. He pulses inside me, prolonging my climax as he fills me to the brim with his potent release.

I collapse against his chest, my body still shuddering through the aftershocks. Ryan holds me close, his heart pounding in tandem with mine as we float down from our mutual high. Boneless and sated, I can't even muster the energy to move, content to stay wrapped up in his strong arms forever.

"I'm never letting you go," he murmurs into my hair, large hands stroking soothingly up and down my back.

That's the last thing I remember before I drift off into a contented sleep.

eight

. . .

Ryan

MY HEART POUNDS as I adjust the fluffy white beard. The weight of the Santa suit feels oppressive, matching the heaviness in my chest. Children's excited squeals echo through the community center as I take my seat on the oversized red velvet throne.

"Ho ho ho!" I boom, forcing cheer into my voice. But inside, I'm drowning in guilt.

Anastasia appears, radiant in a green sweater that highlights her curves. Her smile outshines the twinkling lights as she directs families into neat lines. God, she's beautiful. And I'm lying to her with every breath.

"You're doing great," she whispers, squeezing my shoulder. The warmth of her touch spreads through me.

I nod, not trusting my voice. A little girl climbs onto my lap, rattling off her Christmas list. I listen attentively, but my eyes keep drifting to Anastasia. The way she laughs with parents, comforts crying toddlers. Her compassion knows no bounds.

She would make a great mother. A mother to *our* children. And suddenly I can see it so clearlly. A little girl with Anastasia's eyes, her belly rounded with our second child. She and I cooking together in the kitchen.

My chest tightens. Fuck, I want that.

And then I remember that she could be pregnant with my child even now. A surge of possession rushes through me.

Mine.

Hours pass in a blur of candy canes and childish giggles, and all the while my eyes are glued on my woman.

Finally, we're taking a short break while the other workers entertain the waiting families.

"Ryan," she says softly. "Can we talk?"

My stomach clenches. "Of course."

She takes a deep breath. "I...I think I'm falling for you."

The words I've longed to hear. And they cut like knives.

"You're kind and funny and so giving," she continues. "I've never met anyone like you."

If only she knew the truth. That I'm not who she thinks I am. That I've been deceiving her from the start.

I open my mouth to confess, but the words die on my tongue. I'm a coward.

Instead, I pull her close, breathing in her cinnamon scent. "Anastasia," I murmur. "I—"

But I can't finish. Can't bear to shatter this perfect moment with my lies.

She deserves better. She deserves the truth.

And I'm terrified of losing her when she learns it.

So, instead, I grab Anastasia's hand, pulling her into the dimly lit backroom. My heart thunders as I press her against the wall, devouring her mouth. She moans, fingers tangling in my hair.

"God, I'm *obsessed* with you," I growl, nipping her plump lower lip. My hands roam her lush curves, squeezing her ass.

Anastasia arches into me. "Ryan," she pants. "We shouldn't—the event—"

I silence her with another searing kiss. "Let me taste you, baby. Just for a minute."

She whimpers as I drop to my knees, pushing up her skirt. The scent of her arousal makes my mouth water. I drag my tongue along her thigh, inching higher.

I bury my face between her trembling thighs, lapping at her sweet nectar. Anastasia gasps, fingers tightening in my hair as I devour her slick folds. Her taste explodes on my tongue, intoxicating and addictive. Fuck, my baby is sweeter than a sugar cookie. I could spend eternity worshipping at this altar.

"Oh god, Ryan," she whimpers, hips undulating against my eager mouth. I grip her thighs, spreading her wider, thrusting my tongue deep inside her quivering channel. Her arousal coats my lips and chin. I groan in bliss.

My cock throbs, straining against my red velvet pants. But this is about her pleasure, not mine. I want to make her come apart, shatter in ecstasy.

I circle her swollen clit with the tip of my tongue before suckling the sensitive nub. Anastasia cries out, back arching off the wall. "Yes, yes! Don't stop!"

Her thighs clamp around my head as I flick my tongue faster, massaging her clit. She grinds against my face, chasing her pleasure. I can feel how close she is, inner muscles fluttering.

"Come for me, baby," I command, voice muffled. "Let go. I've got you."

With a keening moan, Anastasia shatters. Her sweet cream gushes into my mouth as she pulses and spasms. I lap up every drop, groaning at the exquisite taste of her release.

Slowly, her tremors subside. I place a tender kiss to her mound before rising to my feet. Anastasia sags against me, boneless and sated. I wrap my arms around her, holding her close.

"That was...incredible," she murmurs dreamily, nuzzling my neck.

Pride surges through me. "I want to give you everything, baby."

But our blissful moment is shattered by a sharp knock at the door. We spring apart, hastily adjusting rumpled clothing.

"Ryan? It's time for the big finale," one of the event coordinators calls.

"Be right there," I reply, voice gravelly.

Anastasia smooths her hair, cheeks flushed. "We should get back out there."

I nod, stealing one last passionate kiss. Then we exit the backroom, trying to look casual.

But my heart stops when I see who's waiting in the crowd. My assistant, Jenna, stands there, eyes wide with shock. And beside her...

"Ryan Caldwell?" Jenna's sister, a local gossip blogger, gapes at me. "The billionaire? What are you doing here?"

Anastasia stiffens, slowly turning to face me. Confusion and betrayal war in her beautiful green eyes.

"Billionaire?" she whispers, voice trembling. "Ryan, what is she talking about?"

I watch helplessly as Anastasia's warm green eyes dawn with comprehension and then hurt, her inviting smile replaced by a trembling frown. She steps back, her curves no longer pressed against me, leaving me aching with loss.

"You lied to me," she whispers, her voice cracking. "All this time..."

I reach for her, desperate. "Anastasia, please—"

She jerks away, wrapping her arms around herself. "Don't touch me. How could you?"

My chest tightens. I've fucked up royally. "I wanted you to know the real me, not my name and anything you may have heard about the ruthless businessman."

Anastasia's laugh is bitter. "The real you? I don't even know who that is anymore."

I step closer, my voice low and urgent. "I'm still the same man who helped you hang Christmas lights. Who listened to you talk about your dreams.

Who kisses you like you're the only woman in the world."

Her eyes flash. "That man wouldn't have lied to me."

"I love you, Ana," I confess, the words bursting from me. "I've never felt this way about anyone. I was scared—"

"Scared?" she interrupts. "Try betrayed. That's how I feel right now."

My heart shatters. I've lost the only thing that truly matters—her trust.

Anastasia's auburn hair swings as she turns, each step widening the chasm between us. My body aches to follow, to gather her softness in my arms and never let go. But I'm frozen, shackled by the weight of my deception.

"Anastasia," I rasp, my voice raw. "Please."

She pauses, her shoulders rigid. When she faces me, her eyes glisten with unshed tears. "I need...time, Ryan. Space."

The sound of my name on her lips—once a caress, now a dagger. I swallow hard. "How long?"

"I don't know." Her voice wavers. "But we've still got an event to handle. You need to get on stage."

My mind races, desperate for the right words to fix this. But there are none. I've shattered something precious, and no amount of wealth can buy it back.

So I do the only thing I can and head onto stage. There's no way in hell I'm going to let my fuck-up ruin's Anastasia's event.

nine

. . .

Ryan

AS SOON AS I CAN, I exit the stage. I scan the bustling crowd, searching for a glimpse of auburn curls and emerald eyes. My heart pounds as I push through the throng of revelers, desperate to find her. But Anastasia is gone, vanished like smoke.

"Damn it," I growl, raking a hand through my hair. How could I have let her slip away? The memory of her hurt expression haunts me. I need to explain, to make things right.

But she clearly wants space. I should respect that. I'm not used to being denied what I want, but

Anastasia isn't some corporate acquisition to be pursued relentlessly. She's...different. Special.

Still, I can't just let her go. Not without a fight.

Back in my hotel suite, I pace like a caged animal. My tech empire has given me nearly unlimited resources. It would be child's play to track her down.

Is it wrong to use those means? To invade her privacy?

"You're doing it to apologize," I mutter. "To fix things."

My fingers fly over my laptop keys. Within minutes, I have her address and phone number.

I memorize the information, chest tight. Now I can reach her. But should I?

The right thing would be to leave her alone. But the thought of never seeing Anastasia again makes me want to put my fist through a wall.

I've never felt this powerless. This conflicted.

My fingers hover over the phone screen, heart pounding. I type out a message, delete it, try again. Nothing feels right. How do you compress regret, longing, and desperation into a text?

Finally, I settle on something simple:

> Anastasia, it's Ryan. Can we talk?
> Please.

I hit send before I can second-guess myself. The message whooshes away, leaving me breathless with anticipation.

Seconds tick by. Minutes. No response.

"Fuck," I mutter, pacing the length of my suite. Each step is agony, my mind replaying her face—those striking green eyes filled with hurt, her soft lips trembling.

I want to taste those lips again. To run my hands through her auburn waves, to feel her curves pressed against me.

But I've ruined it all.

"You're a goddamn idiot, Caldwell," I snarl at my reflection. "You had her in your arms and you let her go."

My phone remains stubbornly silent. No buzz. No chime. Nothing.

I check it again, willing a response to appear. Still nothing.

The urge to throw it against the wall is overwhelming. Instead, I grip it tighter, knuckles white.

"I'm sorry," I whisper to the empty room, imagining Anastasia's warm smile. "I'm so fucking sorry."

———

The clock ticks past midnight. Christmas Eve.

I'm alone in my penthouse, surrounded by opulent holiday decorations that suddenly feel hollow. The twinkling lights mock me, reminding me of the spark in Anastasia's eyes when she talked about her charity work.

"Merry fucking Christmas," I mutter, pouring another whiskey. The amber liquid burns, but it's nothing compared to the ache in my chest.

I slump onto the leather couch, staring at the massive Christmas tree. It's perfect, professionally decorated. Anastasia would hate it. She'd want something homemade, personal. Probably covered in ornaments made by local kids.

God, I can picture her so clearly. Bundled up in one of those soft sweaters she loves, a bright scarf around her neck. Cheeks flushed from the cold as she hangs stockings for the less fortunate.

"You don't deserve her," I growl at myself.

The whiskey glass shatters against the wall. I'm on my feet, pacing again. My fists clench and unclench.

"But I need her."

The admission tears from my throat. Raw. Primal.

I slam my fist into the wall. Pain explodes through my hand, but it's nothing compared to the agony of losing her. I punch again. And again. Drywall crumbles.

"Anastasia," I pant, forehead pressed against the ruined wall.

Blood drips from my knuckles. I welcome the pain. It's better than the emptiness.

ten

. . .

Anastasia

I STARE into the crackling fire, my mind swirling with thoughts of Ryan. Maggie's voice breaks through my reverie.

"Anastasia, honey, you've been a million miles away all evening. What's going on?"

I turn to face my friend, curled up on the other end of the couch. Her concerned eyes search my face.

"It's Ryan," I admit, my voice barely above a whisper. "I can't stop thinking about him."

"The mysterious hottie who turned out to be a billionaire?" Maggie raises an eyebrow.

I nod, twisting my hands in my lap. I googled Ryan. He's known for being cutthroat, ruthless. A lot of people fear him. A lot of people hate him.

But that's not the man I know.

"Finding out about his wealth shocked me at first. But the more I think about it, the more I realize it doesn't change who he is—the man I fell for."

"And who exactly is that man?" Maggie prompts gently.

Images of Ryan flash through my mind—his piercing blue eyes crinkling as he laughs, his strong hands tenderly wrapping gifts for the children's charity drive, the way he looks at me like I'm the only woman in the world.

"He's kind," I say softly. "Thoughtful. Passionate about helping others. When I'm with him, I feel seen in a way I never have before."

My chest tightens as the truth hits me full force. "Oh god, Maggie. I still love him. I love him so much it hurts."

"Then maybe you should tell him that," Maggie says gently.

I nod. Maggie gives me a long hug before she finally leaves me to my solitude.

———

I'm still sitting on the couch, staring at my phone, ready to text Ryan back when thunderous pounding on the front door makes me jump.

Ryan's deep voice carries through the wood, raw with emotion.

"Anastasia! Please, I need to see you. I'm sorry, I tried to stay away, to give you space. But I can't. You're mine, sweetheart. I can't let you go."

My heart races. I drop my phone and rise on shaky legs, drawn to Ryan's voice like a magnet.

I yank open the door, my breath catching at the sight of Ryan. His hair is disheveled, blue eyes blazing with intensity. Before I can speak, he surges forward, cupping my face in his large hands.

"Anastasia, baby," he breathes, his gaze roaming hungrily over my features. "I fucked up. I should've told you everything from the start. But I swear, every moment with you has been real. You're the only thing that matters to me."

My hands tremble as I grasp his wrists. "Ryan, I—"

He cuts me off with a searing kiss, pouring all his desperation and longing into it. I melt against him, my curves fitting perfectly against his hard body. When we break apart, I'm panting.

"I'm dying, baby," his voice breaks. "I can't live without you, honey. I'll give it all up. Donate every fucking cent to charity. I don't care. Just say you're still mine. Let me back into your life."

My heart beats a staccato rythym in my chest.

"I forgive you," I whisper, running my fingers through his hair. "Your heart was always in the right place. That's the man I fell in love with—the one who cares so deeply for others."

Ryan's eyes darken with desire. "Say it again," he growls.

"I love you," I breathe against his lips.

He lifts me effortlessly, kicking the door shut behind us.

Ryan carries me to my bedroom, his lips never leaving mine as he lays me gently on the bed. The Christmas lights twinkle, casting a warm glow on our entwined bodies.

"I can never lose you again, Anastasia," Ryan murmurs fervently against my skin. "You're my life, my everything. Without you, I'm just a shell of a man, going through the motions."

His voice cracks with raw emotion. I cup his face, feeling the rough stubble beneath my palms. "I'm here," I whisper. "I'm not going anywhere. You have me, all of me."

Ryan's eyes glisten, and a single tear escapes, trailing down his chiseled cheek. I catch it with my thumb, my heart swelling with love for this complex, beautiful man.

"I need you," he breathes. "I need to show you how much I love you, how much I cherish you."

His hands slide reverently over my curves, igniting sparks of desire in their wake. He undresses me slowly, worshipping every inch of my body with tender kisses and whispered praises.

"You're so beautiful," he murmurs, his lips grazing the swell of my breasts. "So perfect. I can't believe you're mine."

I arch into his touch, my skin burning with need. "Show me," I plead.

He does, with a gentleness that brings tears to my eyes. His strong body covers mine, his weight a comforting anchor as he joins us together in the most intimate way possible.

This time it's slow, with him looking deep into my eyes and whispering promises in my ear while placing lingering kisses all over my body.

We move as one, our breaths mingling, hands intertwined. The pleasure builds slowly, a delicious tension coiling tighter and tighter until it shatters, sending us both over the edge with cries of ecstasy.

Afterward, we lay tangled together, limbs entwined, hearts beating in sync. Ryan presses soft kisses to my hair, my forehead, my lips.

"I love you," he whispers, his voice thick with emotion. "I'll spend the rest of my life proving it to you, Anastasia. You're my forever."

I snuggle closer, basking in the warmth of his love. "Merry Christmas, Ryan," I murmur sleepily.

He tightens his arms around me, a contented sigh escaping his lips. "Merry Christmas, sweetheart."

epilogue

. . .

Five years later

Ryan

"DADDY, IS SANTA REALLY COMING TONIGHT?" Lily yawns, her green eyes fluttering sleepily, so like her mother's.

I tuck the blanket snug around her little body. "He sure is, pumpkin. And if you go right to sleep, morning will come faster and you'll get to open all the presents he brings."

Anastasia leans down to kiss Lily's forehead, her chestnut hair falling in a silky curtain. "Sweet dreams, baby girl. We love you to the moon and back."

"Love you mostest," Lily mumbles, drifting off.

We slip out quietly, Anastasia's hand finding mine. Five years ago, I never could have imagined this life—a beautiful wife, a perfect daughter, a family to cherish. Anastasia changed everything when her caring heart saw past the ruthless corporate raider to the man I could become. For her. For our daughter

"The addition is really coming along," I say softly go over the latest email about the construction. Expanding the center was Anastasia's greatest wish, and making her dreams reality is my deepest joy.

She squeezes my hand. "I'm so proud of you, Ryan. The way you've transformed your business, always looking out for the little guy now. You're a good man."

I pull her close, inhaling her sweet vanilla scent. "Because of you, darling. You saved my soul." I brush a tender kiss to her temple. "There's nothing I wouldn't do for our family."

And I mean it, with every fiber of my being. They are my world, my reason, my redemption.

But now that our little girl is in bed, it's time for me to take care of my other girl.

I pat my lap, inviting Anastasia to sit on it.

She does obediently.

"Anastasia," I purr, "have you been a good girl this year?"

She blushes, an enchanting flush creeping up her face. She loves this game. We started playing it four Christmases ago, and we've done it every Christmas since. "I think so...?" She licks her lips, and my cock hardens.

"And what do good girls get?" I ask, raising an eyebrow.

"Santa might bring them presents?" she says, biting her lip playfully.

"That's right, baby. So, what does my perfect baby want Santa to give her for Christmas?"

Instead of answering me, Anastasia changes the script, a mischeivous twinkle in her eyes.

She drops to her knees before me.

Oh fuck yes.

My cock grows even harder when I realize her intent.

Anastasia's tongue flicks out, wetting her plump lips. Her hands slide up my thighs, nails leaving delicious trails of heat.

She undoes my pants, and my cock springs free, bobbing in the air between us.

My breath catches when she takes me in her

warm mouth, sucking and licking like I'm the world's best lollipop.

Fuck me.

"Oh, fuck, Ana," I hiss, thrusting my hips into her waiting mouth. She moans around my cock, the vibrations sending shivers down my spine.

I let her play a bit more, but I can never take much of my wife's cocksucking before I blow, and I want to come in her pussy.

"Enough," I finally muster up the control to growl. She whimpers as my cock pops from her mouth, but I shush her as I lift her up and position her on all fours. She looks over her shoulder, that naughty glint in her eyes.

I pull down her festive red panties and slide my fingers through her slick folds. She's dripping wet already, eager and ready for me.

"You want Santa's big candy cane, don't you baby?" I tease, rubbing the swollen head of my cock against her entrance.

"Yes, please Santa!" she begs breathlessly, pushing back against me. "I've been such a good girl, I need it so badly!"

With a low groan, I thrust deep inside her in one smooth stroke. Her tight heat engulfs me and we both moan at the exquisite sensation. I start pumping into her, firm and steady, just how she likes it.

"Oh Ryan, yes! You fill me up so good!" Anastasia cries out as I pound into her sweet spot over and over.

I reach around to rub tight circles on her clit and she bucks wildly against me. "That's it, come on Santa's cock like a good little girl," I growl in her ear.

Her walls clench rhythmically around me as she shatters with a keening cry. I thrust through her orgasm, drawing it out until she's trembling and gasping my name.

"Fuck, Ana, I'm gonna come!" I grit out, my climax cresting.

"Yes, fill me up Ryan! I want to feel you explode inside me!" she urges breathlessly.

A few more deep strokes and I burst, shooting my hot seed deep in her fluttering channel with a primal groan. Wave after wave of ecstasy crashes over me as I empty myself completely, trying my damnedest to get her pregnant again.

I collapse on top of her, both of us panting and sated. I press soft kisses along her neck and shoulder. "I love you so much, Anastasia. You're the best gift I could ever receive. You and Lily."

She turns in my arms to face me, her eyes

shining with love and contentment. "And the new little one on the way."

I go completely still as I look down at her, her words crashing over me. "You're pregnant?"

She smiles radiantly and nods.

My heart explodes with joy. "Oh, baby," my voice cracks with emotion. "You're amazing. You know that, right?"

"I love you too, Ryan," she smiles. "More than anything. Merry Christmas, handsome."

I plant a reverent kiss on her forehead, this perfect, breathtaking woman who's changed my life in so many beautiful ways. "Merry Christmas, baby."

Want a free book from Emma Bray? Go to www. authoremmabray.com.

Keep reading for an excerpt from Rocky Christmas.

Rocky

I take a sip of my club soda as I watch the boxing match on the big screen.

While I'd love to have a beer, that's not what I'm here for. When I'm scheduled to fight in a match, I go through a grueling process of abstinence. I watch my diet. No processed or refined foods. Only healthy, whole foods. No alcohol. No fucking—not that there's been any fucking for me for years. I have two hands to sate my needs with, but I even abstain from self-gratification before a match.

My trainers insist that a strict diet with no drugs of any kind, including alcohol, and no sex helps build up the testosterone needed to really channel a good fight. I don't know how much I believe all that shit, but I do know I want to make sure my body is a well-honed machine when fight time comes around, so I follow their advice.

I'm not much for heavy drink anyway. I prefer to keep a clear head about myself, but a good beer is hard to beat every now and then. After this match, I'll have me one, I silently promise myself as I take another swig of the soda.

"Ooh, that's gotta hurt," the guy to my right says, his eyes glued to the screen. I look back up at the TV as Riker delivers a right hook to his opponent.

I grunt in agreement. My brother sure knows his stuff when it comes to boxing.

I'm glad I was able to talk him into taking it up instead of watching him waste away up on the top of that mountain he lives on. He's only in his early thirties—like me—but he went into the military when we were younger—unlike me. He's never told me what happened over there. All I know is that he came back a different man. He won't talk to me. He won't talk to reporters. Hell, he won't talk to anyone.

Before I turned him on to boxing, he used to just sit up in his house secluded away from everyone, brooding and doing fuck who knows what.

He's got a lot of rage in him. Anyone can tell that by watching him box. You don't box the way he does without having something to work out. At least he has an outlet to channel his frustration into.

I like a good boxing match too, but my strengths lie in MMA. I like the variety. I like the combativeness of it, and while I don't have the aggression and internal turmoil my brother does, I have a passion for the sport.

Riker KO's his opponent a minute later, and pride fills my chest for my brother. The ref holds Riker's hand up, declaring him the champion of the match. My brother accepts the applause, but he doesn't look jubilant like most victors of a fight do. He's just as stoic as usual, with the same grim, no-nonsense expression he's worn since he came back from overseas.

I plop down some money on the bar and stand. Now that the match is over, I can go home and rest up for my own match.

I'm mentally calculating the time difference between my brother and me so that I can figure out when to give him a call to congratulate him on his latest win when I turn around and stop dead in my tracks.

My eyes light on a mass of fiery red hair that tumbles down a slender back. Those red locks almost touch the top of the woman's ass, and I stare at them mesmerized. The locks are full and wild, curling out every which way. I've never been the kind of guy who gets off on hair, but this woman's hair is fucking beautiful. My fingers twitch at my sides. I have the sudden urge to spear my hands into that hair and see if it feels as soft and silky as it looks.

The curls bounce as the girl tips her head back and laughs before she hops off the barstool beside her grinning friend, a brunette who I hardly notice out of the corner of my eyes because my gaze is pinned on the pretty little redhead.

She can't be much more than five feet tall, and when she looks in my direction, my chest tightens like I've been punched in the gut when I look into the prettiest pair of green eyes I've ever seen. They're big and innocent-looking and framed by thick, dark lashes.

I know fucking is on my list of prohibited activities, but I'd break every rule in the book for a chance to get my dick wet by this pretty little redhead, but it's not even about that. I'm not just looking at her in lust, though I'd be lying if I said I'm not practically salivating at the thought of burying myself inside what I already know is going to be the tightest little pussy in the world.

No, it's more than that. I feel something I've never felt before surge inside me when I look at her. I don't just want to stick my dick inside her. I want to wrap her up in my arms and hold her close to me forever. I want to crawl inside her head and learn everything there is to know about her.

I blink when I realize I would be happy just to talk to her. I want to get to know her. There's something about her.

I know that if I ever did get inside her, there's no way I'd ever be able to let her go.

My head should be in the game. I should be mentally prepping myself for my fight tomorrow. A lot of big players have bet money on me. I know that. I don't want to let them down. I don't want to let myself down.

But right now, the only thing I can think about is the pretty little redhead across the bar and finding out what her name is.

I take another sip of my club soda before I plop it back down on the bar. I grimace. Fuck, I wish that was a beer.

I might can abstain from alcohol for the sake of the match, but there's no way I'm going to leave this bar without finding out who this tiny angel is.

———

Holly

Cara's eyes widen as they focus on something behind me.

My laugh dies off, and I turn, my own eyes widening when I see what she sees.

The biggest, burliest man I've ever seen in my entire life is stalking over toward us. A thick, dark brown beard adorns the bottom half of his face. His shirt is molded to the ridges of muscles straining against his T-shirt like it's all the fabric can do to contain all that manliness.

Even though it's winter in Denver, this man is wearing short sleeves like he laughs in the face of the cold weather. Tats decorate his arms.

He's a powerhouse of masculinity.

Good lord, what does this man do? Weight-lift cars?

All that muscle must be more than enough to protect him against winter's chill, but I'm wrapped up in a turtleneck sweater. I'm also wearing a big, fluffy coat too. I stay cold all the time, but this man…something tells me that his big body is like a furnace.

I'm proved correct when he finally stops right in front of me—so close to me that there's scarcely an inch left between our bodies. I tip my head up to look at the giant towering over me. I'm barely five foot two, so I'm short even compared to the average person, but this guy is way above average. He has to be well over six feet tall, making me appear even teenier and tinier than usual.

His eyes are a deep brown, like the finest chocolate.

They bore down into me in a way that sends all the blood rushing to my cheeks.

His eyes have taken mine captive. I couldn't look away from them if I tried.

I vaguely register Cara murmuring something, but I can't make out what she's saying over the roaring in my ears. It's like this man has caused everything around me to dim.

The man's eyes rove over my face as if he's trying to commit all of it to memory before one of his giant hands reach out to gently touch my hair.

His lips part slightly, and my breath hitches.

"What's your name, sweetheart?" His voice is like a big rumble of thunder, and it sends little shock waves rolling through me.

"Holly." I don't even contemplate not answering him because I'm suddenly dying to know who he is too.

I don't even have to prompt him for his own name.

"Holly," he tastes my name on his lips and nods his head in approval.

My blush deepens, pleasure unfurling deep in my belly at the look of approval on his face.

"I'm Rocky," that deep voice rumbles again.

"Rocky," I repeat his name like he did mine, and his eyes close for a moment as if he's savoring the sound of it.

"Say it again," he rumbles.

My cheeks flame even brighter, but I give him what he wants.

"Rocky."

A shudder goes through his big frame. "I've never liked the sound of my name so much," he growls before he pins me in his intense gaze again.

He takes a deep breath before he says, his eyes never leaving mine, "I'm not good with subterfuge, Holly. I'm not one of those guys who's going to dance around what he wants and ease into it. I see what I want, and I go after ut."

My heart beats against my ribcage as the intensity in his eyes deepens.

"When I saw you across the room just now…" He shakes his big head before he continues. "I don't know what happened, but fuck, I want you."

My breath catches.

He rushes on, "I know I'm coming on strong, and I don't want to freak you out, but I don't see any point in beating around the bush. I'm going to make you mine."

The way he says *mine* comes out as a growl, and my heart flutters at the possessive way he's looking at me—like I already belong to him.

This is crazy. I don't know anything about this guy, and I've never wanted to belong to someone before. A monologue like this coming from any other man would undoubtedly infuriate me. It would come off as cocky and arrogant, but it doesn't come off that way with this man.

I get the sense that this isn't just some line he uses, that he's speaking from his soul.

And I'm loving the sound of him making me *his*.

It calls to me on a primal level. Even though he's the biggest, scariest-looking man I've ever seen, I also somehow feel completely safe in his presence—like nothing could ever hurt me.

When I don't speak, he runs a hand through his hair, a look of regret and self-loathing on his face.

"Fuck, I've just scared the shit out of you."

Frustration pours off him. He looks like he wishes he could beat himself up.

I instinctively want to soothe him. I lay a hand on his big arm, my fingers trembling atop his muscles.

He instantly stills, his eyes flicking up to mine and his chest heaving up and down at my touch. His nostrils flare, but I keep my hand on his arm. I feel like I'm calming a big beast. It both humbles me and empowers me at the same time. Seeing what I do to him almost makes me dizzy.

"You haven't scared me." I shake my head. "It's

just...no one has ever said these things to me before."

He visibly relaxes before he covers my hand with his own. "Let me get to know you." His voice is gruff, and it scrapes over me like sandpaper. "We can go as slow as you want. I just want to spend some time with you, get to know you."

He fingers my hair again, a look of wonder in his eyes. "You're the most beautiful little thing I've ever seen," he murmurs.

My heart races again. He's looking at me like I'm the most precious thing he's ever seen. No one has ever looked at me this way before.

As the senator's daughter, I haven't dated much. I've always been so cautious. I've always had to be careful of who I'm seeing with so it doesn't look bad on my father or his career. I've never dated anyone who wasn't vetted and approved by him. My whole life has been planned out around my dad's career.

I've been complacent. I've never done anything just for me in all of my twenty-one years.

As Rocky's eyes bore down into mine, I realize that I'm tired of living that way. I want to do something for me.

I want Rocky. He's going to be that something just for me.

I'm tired of only dating the guys my dad sets me up with because their connections will further his career. I want to be with someone who wants me just for *me* and not what a connection with my father can do for them.

Rocky doesn't have a clue who I am. That much is obvious.

And that's why I'm not going to tell him my last name. I don't want to ruin this before it ever even begins.

My pulse races as I do the first thing I've ever done just for myself. "I want to get to know you, too."

Get Rocky Christmas here: Rocky Christmas.

www.ingramcontent.com/pod-product-compliance
Lightning Source LLC
Chambersburg PA
CBHW062227150726
47991CB00006B/2470